Hi there!
Max and Ruby say hello.
This book was signed by

Rosemary Wells

March 1993

ROSEMARY WELLS
Max's Chocolate Chicken

SCHOLASTIC INC.
New York Toronto London Auckland Sydney
Mexico City New Delhi Hong Kong

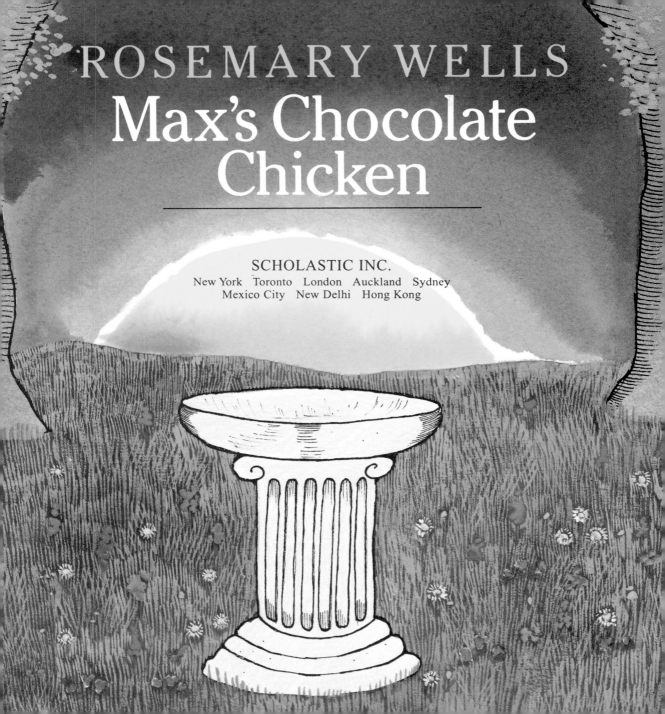

For Janet, who helped enormously

ISBN 0-439-07774-5

Copyright © 1989 by Rosemary Wells.
All rights reserved.
Published by Scholastic Inc., 555 Broadway, New York, NY 10012,
by arrangement with Dial Books for Young Readers,
a division of Penguin Books USA Inc.
SCHOLASTIC and associated logos are trademarks and/or registered
trademarks of Scholastic Inc.

12 11 10 9 8 7 6 5 4 3 2 1   9/9 0 1 2 3 4/0

Printed in the U.S.A.   24

Designed by Atha Tehon
The full-color artwork for each picture
consists of a blank ink drawing and a watercolor wash.

One morning somebody put
a chocolate chicken in the birdbath.

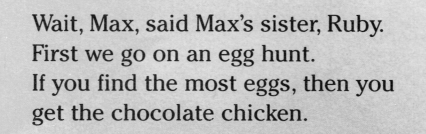

Wait, Max, said Max's sister, Ruby.
First we go on an egg hunt.
If you find the most eggs, then you
get the chocolate chicken.

And if I find the most eggs, then I get the chocolate chicken, said Ruby.

Max went looking for eggs,
but all he found was a mud puddle.

Ruby found a big yellow egg.
Max didn't find any.
No eggs, no chicken, Max, said Ruby.

Max went looking again,
but all he found were acorns.

Ruby found a blue egg.
Max, said Ruby, pull yourself together.
Otherwise you'll never get the chocolate chicken.

So Max went looking with Ruby.
Ruby found a red egg with green stars.
Max found a spoon.

Ruby found a gold egg with purple stripes and a turquoise egg with silver swirls and a lavender egg with orange polka dots. Max found some ants.

Then he made ant-and-acorn pancakes. Max, said Ruby, you'd have trouble finding your own ears if they weren't attached to your head.

Ruby counted her eggs.
I'm the one who's going to get the
chocolate chicken, Max, said Ruby.

But Max ran away.

And hid.

The birdbath was empty.

Where are you, Max? Ruby called.
Max ate the chicken's tail.

I see you, Max! said Ruby.
But she didn't.
Max ate the chicken's head.

I'll give you half the chocolate chicken, Max! yelled Ruby. Max ate the wings.

Then he popped out of his hiding place.

Max, said Ruby, how could you do this to me?

I love you! said Max.